For all the tribe

– L.J.

Dla Babci i Dziadzia

– B.B.

Published in 1995 by Magi Publications
55 Crowland Avenue, Hayes, Middlesex UB3 4JP

Text © 1995 by Linda Jennings
Illustrations © 1995 by Basia Bogdanowicz

The right of Linda Jennings to be identified as the author
of this work has been asserted by her in accordance with
The Copyright, Designs and Patents Act 1988.

Printed and bound in Belgium by Proost N.V. Turnhout

ISBN 1 85430 275 2 (Hardback)
ISBN 1 85430 127 6 (Paperback)

Fred

by
Linda Jennings

illustrated by
Basia Bogdanowicz

MAGI PUBLICATIONS

London

Dad had made Fred a special little door.
Katie told him he could go through it into
the garden.
Fred wasn't sure.
He looked through the cat flap . . .

OH!

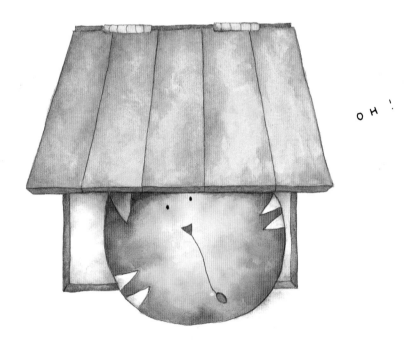

. . . and Horrible Harry from next door was outside!

HA HA!

'Ssss,' said Fred, feeling
very safe. 'Can't catch me!'

WHAM!
Horrible Harry's big paw shot
through the cat flap –
and the flap hit Fred.
'Ouch!' yowled Fred.

Fred hid behind the fridge.
Would Horrible Harry come in?

Horrible Harry tried,
but Katie's mum shooed him away.

'I don't like my cat flap,' said Fred.
'Not if Horrible Harry can come into
my kitchen, just like that.'

'Mieow!' said Fred, a bit later.

He wanted to go out into the garden.

'Use your cat flap,' said Katie.

She pushed at it to show him how.

MEOW!

Fred scratched at the flap with his paws.
It was all slippery and shiny.
It waggled, but it didn't open.
Then Fred pushed at it with his head.
It started to open.

Was Horrible Harry still out there?

Fred jumped back . . .

. . . and the flap jumped back, too!

'I *hate* my flap!' said Fred.

At last Katie pushed Fred through the flap.
'Out you go!' she said. 'It's easy when
you know how.'
'Ow!' yelled Fred.
The cat flap had bitten his tail!

Fred shot across the lawn and hid under
the bushes – just in case Horrible Harry
was still around.

B Z Z Z !

Fred stayed hidden
for a very long time.
He began to feel hungry.

'Come on, Fred, suppertime,' called Katie's
mum at last. She stood outside with a plate
of catfood.
Horrible Harry was sitting on the wall.
'Should I risk it?' thought Fred.

SHHH!

Fred crawled out.

He hoped Horrible Harry wouldn't
see him.

Then, just as he reached the door,
Katie's mum went inside and shut it.

USE YOUR FLAP !

'Use your flap,' she called out to him.
But Fred was frightened to go through,
in case it bit his tail again.

Fred hid behind a flowerpot.

By now he was very *very* hungry.

When Katie's mum next opened the door,

Fred slipped in.

'You naughty kitten,' said Katie's mum.
'You'll never use your cat flap if you
don't try.'

SHAME !

Fred decided to try very hard.

He stood at the far end of the kitchen,
shut his eyes and ran very fast towards the
cat flap . . .

. . . and hurtled through it,
like a furry bullet . . .

MEEE OOOW!

. . . right into the garden –
where Horrible Harry was waiting
for him!

YIPPEE!

Horrible Harry didn't
know what had hit him,
and he didn't stop to find out.
He fled over the wall into his own garden.
'My cat flap is brilliant!' said Fred.